MY - '22

To my children, Soleil and Amani—B. P.
For Rohan—Adventure Awaits!—J. A.

BAPTISTE PAUL is a children's picture book author. His first book for NorthSouth, *The Field*, received three starred reviews and won the Sonia Lynn Sadler Award, was a Junior Library Guild selection, and also appeared on *The Horn Book* Fanfare Best of 2018, the *School Library Journal* Best of 2018, and the CCBC 2018 Choices lists. Baptiste is also the coauthor of *Peace* (Baptiste Paul and Miranda Paul, illustrated by Estelí Meza), which received a starred review from *SLJ*. Baptiste loves sports, likes to roast his own coffee, and grills. He lives in Wisconsin with his family.

JACQUELINE ALCÁNTARA is the critically acclaimed illustrator of *The Field*, also by Baptiste Paul, which won the Sonia Lynn Sadler Award, was a Junior Library Guild selection, and appeared on *The Horn Book Fanfare* Best of 2018; *Freedom Soup* by New York Times Best Seller Tami Charles which was named a Kids Indie Next and *Junior Library Guild* selection; *Your Mama* by NoNieqa Ramos, which was a finalist for *The Kirkus Prize*, and *Jump at the Sun* by Newbery Honoree Alicia D. Williams, which received multiple starred reviews. You can find her online at her website jacquelinealcantara.com, on Instagram @_jacqueline_ill or biking around Detroit, Michigan where she currently lives.

CLIMB ON!

Written by **Baptiste Paul**

Illustrated by **Jacqueline Alcántara**

North South

Morning, Dad!

Morning!
It's a great day for
watching *futbol*.

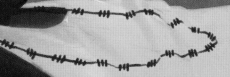

Hmmm! No,
it's a great day for the hike.
Remember?!

To the tippy top?

Daddy, it's called the summit!

Pawe? Ready?

Wait!
I'll double-check the list.

We fill our backpacks.
Water
Snacks!
First Aid Kit
Camera

Courage?

I have courage for two!
Annou ale! Off we go!

Come on, Dad!

It starts as soon
as we set foot on the
BIG stone steps.

Are we there yet?

Finally!

Which way?

Dwèt. Right.

Góch. Left.

This path? No.

That path? Maybe.

Our shadows disappear
under a shaded canopy.

Which way now?

Buzz, buzz, buzz.
Smack, smack, smack!

Hmmm . . . turn back?

No way!

Mouté. Climb on.

Swing. Swing.

Wheeeeeeee!!!!! Want to try?

Maybe next time . . .

Mouté! Climb on!

The only way to the summit
is up this ladder?

Hang on and hold tight.

Step.

Breathe.

Sweat.

Burn.

Are we there yet?

No way!
We're only halfway.

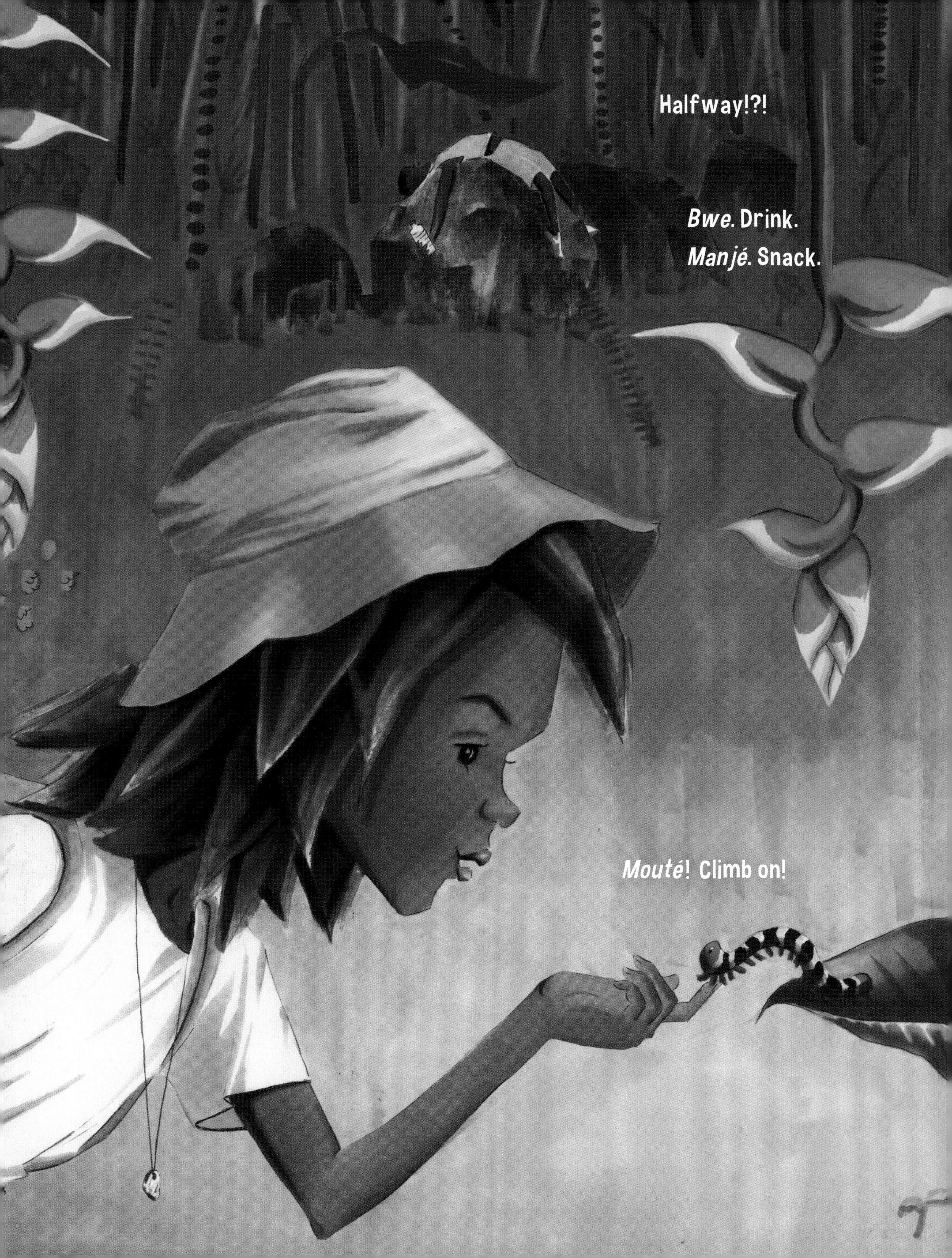

Halfway!?!

Bwe. Drink.
Manjé. Snack.

Mouté! Climb on!

The rocks weep from yesterday's rain.
Each step slower than the last.

Fé vit. Hurry up!
Step.
Breathe.
Sweat.

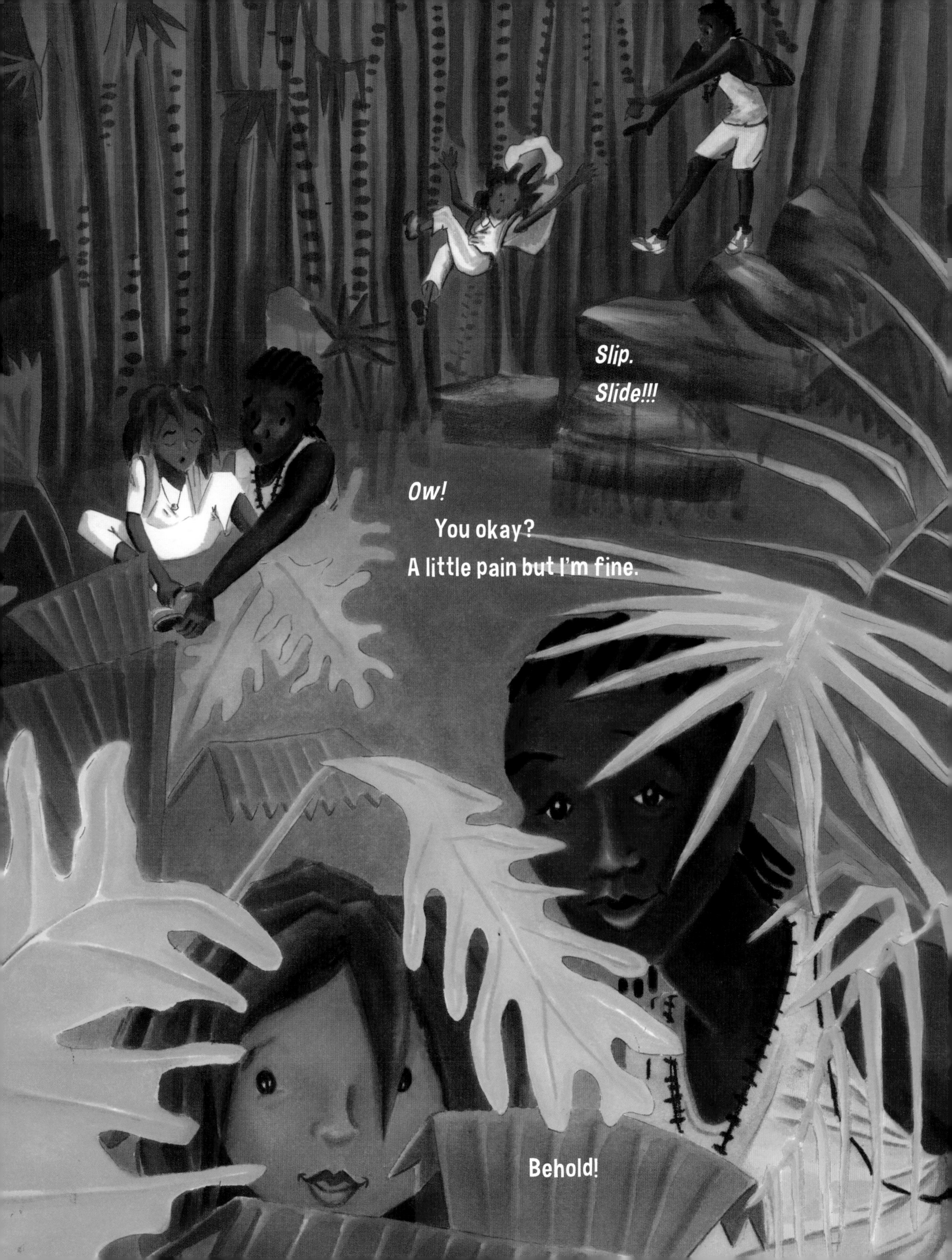
Slip.
Slide!!!
Ow!
You okay?
A little pain but I'm fine.
Behold!

The town!
A mosaic masterpiece.

Indeed!

Mwen las. I'm tired.

Almost there!

Anlé, anlé, anlé.
Up, up, up.

Lanmén. Hand.

Hadi. Pull.

Climb on!

Step.
    Breathe.
Sweat.
    Burn.

Step.
    Breathe.
Sweat.
    Steep! (Eep!)

Camera? Uh-oh.
Can't find it.
Click! Click!
Chonjé. Remember.

Wow.